TWO BEARS
at the party

Story by Cathie and David Bell

Pictures by Jan Brychta

Oxford University Press

For Emily

Oxford University Press, Walton Street, Oxford OX2 6DP

Oxford New York Toronto
Delhi Bombay Calcutta Madras Karachi
Petaling Jaya Singapore Hong Kong Tokyo
Nairobi Dar es Salaam Cape Town
Melbourne Auckland

and associated companies in
Berlin Ibadan

Oxford is a trade mark of Oxford University Press

The Two Bears Books are:

Two Bears at the seaside
Two Bears in the snow
Two Bears at the party
Two Bears go fishing
Two Bears find a pet
Two Bears and the fireworks

Winston and Stanley got an invitation.
It was Emily's birthday.
She was having a fancy dress party.
Everyone had to go as a pirate.

Winston and Stanley went to the fancy dress shop.
They tried on lots of pirate clothes.

Winston put a black patch over his eye.
He looked very fierce.
Stanley found a big pirate hat, and a
little scarf for their pet mouse, Clementine.

When they got home they looked for Clementine.
They showed her their pirate clothes.

'What's Clementine eating?' said Winston.
'Oh no!' said Stanley. 'It's the party invitation!'
'Never mind,' said Winston. 'I can
remember what it said.'

The day of the party came.
Winston and Stanley were very excited.
They put on their pirate clothes and
they set off in the go-kart.
Clementine sat on Winston's shoulder.

'What number is Emily's house?' said Stanley.
'Oh dear,' said Winston, 'it was on the invitation.
I don't think I can remember it after all!'

They knocked on a door.
'We've come to the fancy dress party,' said Winston.
'It's not here,' said the man, 'but I saw lots
of children in fancy dress going into number ten.
Try there.'

They knocked on the door of number ten.
'Is this Emily's Pirate Party?' said Winston.
'No,' giggled the children, 'this is Jake's Clown Party.
Emily lives at number fifteen.'

The two bears went to number fifteen.
Emily's mum opened the door.
'Oh dear,' she said, 'you're too late.
The party was yesterday.'

Winston and Stanley were very sad.
'We have missed the party and now we'll never
be pirates,' said Stanley.
'I'm sorry,' said Winston.

The bears went home.
They took off their pirate clothes.
Stanley put the kettle on.
Suddenly there was a knock at the door.

It was Emily and all her friends.
They were dressed as pirates!
'We heard how sad you were,' said Emily,
'so we're going to have another party –
just for you!'

The bears put on their pirate clothes again.
They played pirate games, and sang pirate songs.
Then they all sat down and ate a pirate tea.
Winston and Stanley were the happiest
pirates in the world!